Bath · New York · Cologne · Melbourne · Delhi
Hong Kong · Shenzhen · Singapore

A world filled with ideas, hope and potential will always attract a great many villains.

But for every villain that attacks, there is a hero to defeat them....

Iron Man is known to the world as billionaire genius Tony Stark. Tony built the suit for himself. His special chest plate keeps his injured heart beating and powers the suit. People say the armour makes him powerful …

… some might even say invincible.

Tony is not the only Super Hero.

Natasha Romanoff spent years training to be a top secret spy, handling missions some thought to be myth.

Eventually, Natasha was recruited by Nick Fury and S.H.I.E.L.D., where she was given high-tech equipment and the code name 'Black Widow'.

And Black Widow can always rely on Hawkeye.

Orphaned at an early age, Clint Barton worked for a travelling circus as a master archer. After witnessing Iron Man rescue people in danger, Clint knew that he too wanted to be a Super Hero and help those in need.

Clint made a costume and a range of trick arrows, equipped with exploding tips, stunners and electrical nets. He became known as Hawkeye and joined the mighty Avengers.

And when Hawkeye's arrows aren't enough, there is always ...
the Hulk!

After being exposed to gamma radiation, scientist Bruce Banner
spent most of his life on the run. He always tried to stay calm
because sometimes his emotions could get the better of him....

Banner can transform into a huge green hero, who's always ready
to save the day. But no matter how much he tries to help, people find
it very hard to trust him. So the Hulk mostly keeps to himself.

Born into royalty Thor had earned his honour with acts of bravery and strength. With his mighty hammer, Thor was a force of power capable of summoning lightning, rain and thunder. His brother Loki was angry with him because he wanted to rule Asgard. So Thor imprisoned his brother in a place called the Isle of Silence.

Loki didn't take this well. He wanted revenge!

Loki used his powers to search the Earth – a place his brother loved and had sworn to protect – to find someone people feared. Someone they distrusted. But, above all, someone who could defeat his brother, Thor.

Loki soon found someone – the Incredible Hulk!

The master of mischief, Loki, used his powers to trick the Hulk into believing a high-speed train was about to crash on a broken train track.

The Hulk stopped the train, thinking he had saved the day.

But the broken track was just an illusion. The people on the train thought the Hulk was trying to hurt them. Word spread fast – the Hulk was on a rampage!

And it didn't take long for the news to reach Earth's Mightiest.

Soon the most powerful heroes in the world raced off to save the day.

But Loki had only wanted to lure Thor there, not the others! The Hulk might have been able to crush Thor, but he wouldn't stand a chance against four Super Heroes.

Loki used his powers again to create a version of the Hulk that only Thor could see. Then Loki returned to Asgard, and Thor chased after the fake Hulk!

But when Thor tried to strike the Hulk, his mighty hammer went right through him.

"An illusion!" Thor said – and he knew it could only be the work of Loki. Thor rushed back to Asgard and confronted his brother. Like the true coward he was … Loki ran.

But Thor grabbed Loki and brought him down to Earth once again. Thor found the other heroes. They had cornered the real Hulk, who still thought he had done something wrong. Thor dropped Loki into the middle of the battle.

"Thou must know – this is your true villain! My brother, Loki of Asgard, tricked you into believing our comrade, the Hulk, smashed the train!"

And with that, Loki used his magic against the heroes. He created
multiple illusions of himself. The Avengers didn't know which was the
real Loki, so they attacked them all.

But one hero would not be tricked ... the Hulk!

The group liked working together. They realized that, as individuals, they were just Super Heroes. But as a team, they were a mighty, unstoppable force! So they became …

the Avengers!

So whenever big threats arose, the Avengers assembled.
Because there will always be villains in the world....

Some time later, after battling Namor, the Prince of Atlantis, the Avengers were cruising through the Arctic circle in their submarine.

Soon, they spotted something floating in the distance. It looked like something frozen in a block of ice!

The Incredible Hulk swam to the figure and took it back to the sub. He took the block to the medical bay. There was a man trapped inside!

Iron Man slowly thawed the ice, to reveal …

... Captain America! The famous Super-Soldier from World War II!

Cap had saved the world from the evil organization HYDRA and its leader, Red Skull. A failed mission left Cap trapped in ice, but he had survived in suspended animation!

Confused and on guard, Cap listened to the Avengers explain what had happened. They told him they were friends.

But before the group could get too friendly, the sub suddenly shook.

Namor was back and he'd brought an army of Atlanteans with him!

The Avengers fought hard, but they were no match for an entire army. They were overwhelmed.

But then someone who was not an Avenger stepped in ...

… and the tide began to turn! The Avengers, together
with Captain America, defeated Namor and his army.
They had stopped him from waging war on the surface world.
   They were proud of the way they had worked together.
   The final member of their team was in place. Captain America
raised his shield and the others rallied around him.

A new team had been born: Thor, Hulk, Hawkeye, Black Widow, Iron Man … and now, Captain America!
The world would soon realize this group was something mighty.

And if a threat were ever to arise that was too big for one hero …

the Avengers would assemble!